W9-CAW-596

R2-D2 AND C-3PO'S GUIDE TO THE GALAXY

IF I TOLD YOU HALF THE THINGS I KNEW ABOUT THE GALAXY, YOU'D PROBABLY SHORT-CIRCUIT!

SCHOLASTIC INC.

LEGO, the LEGO logo, the Brick and Knob configurations and the Minifigure are trademarks of the LEGO Group. © 2016 The LEGO Group. Produced by Scholastic Inc. under license from The LEGO Group.

© & TM 2016 LUCASFILM LTD. Used Under Authorization.

All rights reserved. Published by Scholastic Inc., *Publishers since 1920.* SCHOLASTIC and associated logos are trademarks and/or registered trademarks of Scholastic Inc.

The publisher does not have any control over and does not assume any responsibility for author or third-party websites or their content.

No part of this publication may be reproduced, stored in a retrieval system, or transmitted in any form or by any means, electronic, mechanical, photocopying, recording, or otherwise, without written permission of the publisher. For information regarding permission, write to Scholastic Inc., Attention: Permissions Department, 557 Broadway, New York, NY 10012.

This book is a work of fiction. Names, characters, places, and incidents are either the product of the author's imagination or are used fictitiously, and any resemblance to actual persons, living or dead, business establishments, events, or locales is entirely coincidental.

ISBN 978-0-545-94894-4

10 9 8 7 6 5 4 3 2 1   16 17 18 19 20

Printed in China   95
First printing 2016

Book design by Erin McMahon

INTRODUCTION

I AM MOST CERTAINLY NOT BABBLING ON TOO LONG, YOU PESKY ASTROMECH. NOW, LET ME BEGIN THE REAL STORY.

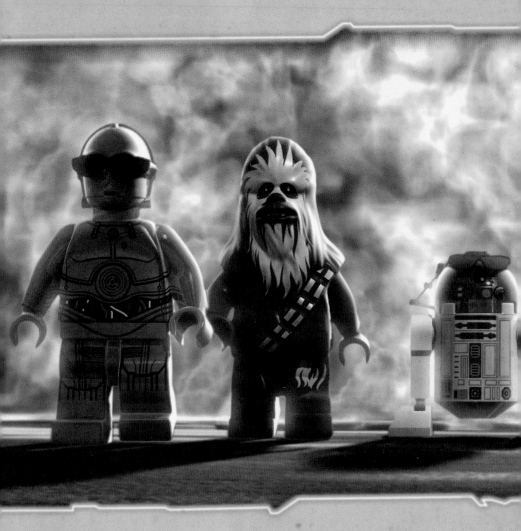

THE REBEL ALLIANCE is a group united against the evil Galactic Empire. Their goal is to remove Emperor Palpatine, aka Darth Sidious, from power and usher in the return of the Galactic Republic. This will allow all the planets to work

ALLIANCE

together to make a better galaxy. Filled with castaways, rogues, and well-trained military, the Rebel Alliance fights for freedom. But with Sith Lords, stormtroopers, and the dark side of the Force in their way, the battle is far from over.

LUKE SKYWALKER

Raised on the desert planet Tatooine, Luke Skywalker has no idea that he is destined for galactic greatness. With the help of Obi-Wan Kenobi, Luke learns to channel the Force and begins his Jedi training. Armed with two droids and his father's lightsaber, Luke starts his journey. Upon befriending Han Solo and saving Princess Leia Organa, Luke joins the Rebel Alliance and defeats the Empire's Death Star. But during his Jedi training with the great Master Yoda, Luke learns that his family has a strong connection to the dark side of the Force.

Luke believes that his father was a Jedi Knight who was defeated by Darth Vader. The truth is that Luke's father, Anakin Skywalker, is actually the very same man who turned against the Jedi Order, joined the dark side, and donned a black mask and helmet to live the rest of his life as the Sith Lord known as Darth Vader.

When faced with a decision to join the dark side with his father, Luke chose to remain a true Jedi and in doing so, defeated the Emperor and dealt the final blow to the Empire.

PRINCESS LEIA ORGANA

Princess Leia is a clever diplomat from Alderaan who is not afraid to stand up to the evil Empire. She's tough, determined, always speaks her mind, and is an active participant in many major rebel missions. Whether it's carrying the stolen plans to destroy the first Death Star or fighting in the Battle of Endor, Leia fears no danger.

Born to the fallen Jedi Knight Anakin Skywalker and Queen Padmé Amidala, Leia is the twin sister of Luke Skywalker. The children were split up and never knew their birth parents or each other, until they met on board the Death Star. Together again, they are the Rebellion's new hope.

BEEP, BRRRRR, WHIRRRRR, BLINK-O-BOP-O-BOOP.

WE KNOW, WE KNOW. LEIA TRUSTED *YOU* WITH THE SECRET TO DESTROYING THE DEATH STAR. I'VE BEEN ON PLENTY OF IMPORTANT MISSIONS AND YOU DON'T SEE ME BRAGGING, SHOW-OFF.

HAN SOLO

Han Solo is a smuggler turned member of the Rebel Alliance after Luke Skywalker and Obi-Wan Kenobi hired him for a mission that turned into the rescue of Princess Leia. Solo is the self-proclaimed best pilot in the universe. Along with his ship, the *Millennium Falcon*, and his trusty copilot, Chewbacca, Solo can back up this claim, having dodged through asteroid fields, made the Kessel Run in less than twelve parsecs, and helped destroy both the first and second Death Stars. But Han's past catches up with him when Boba Fett, a bounty hunter hired by Jabba the Hutt, captures and freezes him in carbonite at Cloud City. With the help of his friends, Han escapes and lives to fight another day!

CHEWBACCA

Chewbacca, also known as Chewie, is a Wookiee from the forest planet Kashyyyk. Early on, he forged a strong friendship with Han Solo and together the two of them went on many adventures in the *Millennium Falcon*. Tall and hairy all over, Chewie looks like a beast, but he is also one of the most caring, wise, and loyal beings in the galaxy. He is also a great mechanic, which is helpful when your ship breaks down as much as Han Solo's does.

OBI-WAN KENOBI

Obi-Wan Kenobi is a great Jedi Knight and well-respected mentor to both Anakin and Luke Skywalker. Nearly as wise as Master Yoda and as powerful as Mace Windu, Obi-Wan fought in the Clone Wars and served on the Jedi High Council. Kenobi is also one of the few Jedi Knights to have faced off against Darth Maul, Count Dooku, General Grievous, Jango Fett, and Anakin Skywalker, proving that he is one of the fiercest warriors in the galaxy.

YODA

Standing at just over two feet tall, Yoda might not look like a great warrior, but this powerful Jedi Master proves that size matters not. Yoda is a leader on the Jedi High Council and an expert in the ways of the Force. Yoda is also a revered teacher, having played an important role in training almost all of the Jedi in the Order, including Obi-Wan Kenobi, Qui-Gon Jin, and Luke Skywalker.

ALTHOUGH I AM PROGRAMMED TO SPEAK MILLIONS OF LANGUAGES, A HARD TIME STILL, I HAVE, UNDERSTANDING YODA.

MACE WINDU

A Jedi Master from Haruun Kal, Mace Windu is second only to Yoda as both a leader and a defender of the Force. Mace is an excellent swordsman, having created his own type of lightsaber combat called Vaapad. Fighting is always a last option for Mace, who prefers to use his wisdom and words to solve issues.

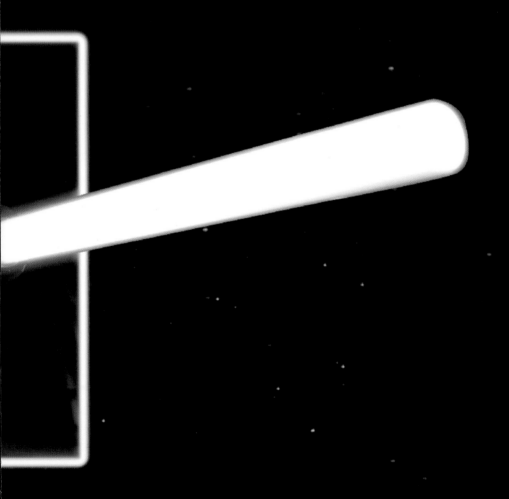

C-3PO

C-3PO is a protocol droid programmed to know everything about etiquette and diplomatic affairs. He is fluent in over six million languages and is constantly worried about everything. Scaredy-droid or not, C-3PO played an important role in some of the most important moments of galactic history. From being rebuilt by a young Anakin Skywalker to serving a young Luke Skywalker, C-3PO is never far away from trouble and adventure . . . even though he hates trouble and adventure.

R2-D2

This astromech droid is strong-willed, courageous, and resourceful. Housed inside his robot frame, R2-D2 has many gadgets that can help with any task from putting out fires to repairing starships. R2-D2 loves a good adventure, whether it's relaying a secret message to Obi-Wan Kenobi or serving as Luke Skywalker's copilot when he destroys the Death Star. This little droid is as brave and tough as they come.

I WOULD LIKE TO ADD TO THIS DESCRIPTION STUBBORN, TROUBLESOME, AND FULL OF FINE MESSES HE ALWAYS GETS US IN. ALSO, HE IS MY BEST FRIEND.

JAR JAR BINKS

Jar Jar Binks is a Gungan from the planet Naboo. He fought alongside the great Jedi Qui-Gon Jinn during the invasion of Naboo and plays a pivotal role in helping the Jedi save Queen Amidala. Not much of a fighter, Jar Jar Binks is naive and clumsy, but has a heart of gold.

QUI-GON JINN

Qui-Gon Jinn is an extraordinary Jedi. He is very well respected, but also has a history of being a maverick. For example, he trained Count Dooku, who later turned to the dark side of the Force. He also trained the great Jedi Obi-Wan Kenobi. But Qui-Gon is best known for discovering Anakin Skywalker. It is upon his insistence that the Jedi Order allows Anakin to be trained in the ways of the Force.

ADMIRAL ACKBAR

Admiral Ackbar is a rebel military commander best known for leading the Alliance attack that destroyed the second Death Star. Originally from the planet Mon Cala, Ackbar is part of an amphibious race known as the Mon Calamari. He is a great military planner, but he is also a stellar pilot who can fly through the underwater world of his home planet just as easily as he zips through space while fighting the Galactic Empire's warship fleet. Always quick with a booming laugh and a positive attitude, Admiral Ackbar is a shining example of the heart and spirit of the Rebel Alliance.

PERSONALLY, THE ADMIRAL FLIES TOO FAST FOR MY TASTE. AND HE NEVER AVOIDS TRAPS!

PADMÉ AMIDALA

Padmé Amidala's full title is Her Royal Highness Queen Amidala of Naboo, and she is, as the name suggests, the Queen of Naboo. She served in the Galactic Senate as one of the most respected politicians in the galaxy. Full of hope, positivity, and a will to do what is right, Padmé fell in love with and married Anakin Skywalker. Together they had two children: the twins, Luke and Leia. Both children inherited Queen Amidala's faith and compassion.

WEDGE ANTILLES

Wedge Antilles is part of the Rebel Alliance and one of their best pilots. He flew alongside Luke Skywalker and Han Solo to help destroy the Death Star in the Battle of Yavin. He is also a member of Rogue Squadron at the Battle of Hoth, and took part in the Battle of Endor. As if that wasn't enough, this flying ace also backed up Lando Calrissian in the rebels' attack on the second Death Star. He is a confident leader and an artist in the cockpit of an X-wing fighter.

LANDO CALRISSIAN

Lando is a smuggler, a gambler, and a con man, but that doesn't mean he's a bad guy. The owner of the *Millennium Falcon* before Han Solo, Lando won the ship in a game of cards. Of course, then he lost it to his friend Han. A classy, well-dressed gentleman in appearance, Lando always has a trick up his sleeve, whether it's helping Darth Vader capture Han or helping Luke Skywalker save Han. He is a crook and a hero all at once, which makes him the perfect addition to the Rebel Alliance.

I DON'T WANT TO TRUST LANDO, BUT HOW CAN YOU SAY NO TO SOMEONE WHO LOOKS THIS COOL?

THE JEDI ORDER

MACE WINDU

KIT FISTO

PLO KOC

OBI-WAN KENOBI

YODA

The Jedi Order is a peacekeeping group that also strives to stop the spread of the dark side of the Force. Led by a Jedi Council, these Jedi Knights are the guardians of peace and justice throughout the galaxy.

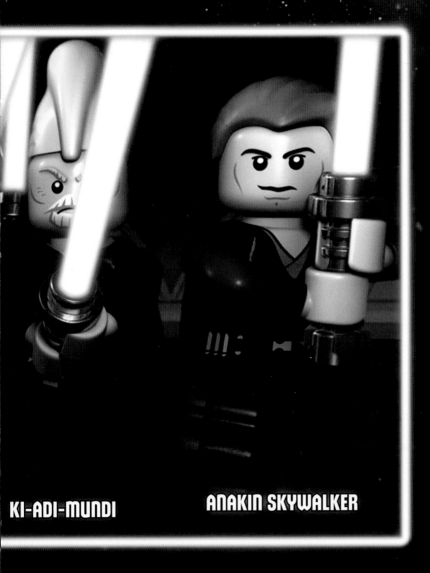

KI-ADI-MUNDI

ANAKIN SKYWALKER

KANAN JARRUS

Kanan Jarrus is overconfident, sarcastic, and head-strong, which might not seem like the best qualities for a Jedi to have, but they make him an excellent rebel. Good with a lightsaber, Kanan is a scrapper of a fighter, having limited training in the art of dueling. A former Padawan, Kanan moves through life keeping his past to himself. But when Ezra joins the crew of the *Ghost*, Kanan realizes that his past is what made him the man he is today, and he reconnects with his Jedi abilities in order to take down the Empire.

EZRA BRIDGER

Hailing from the planet Lothal, Ezra Bridger is a street-smart kid who also happens to be unexpectedly Force-sensitive. He has lived on his own as a con artist since the age of seven. In fact, when he joined the rebel crew aboard the *Ghost*, Ezra had planned on stealing the group's valuables. But after learning of his Jedi nature and befriending the other rebels, Ezra decided to stay and join their fight.

> I LIKE THIS KID. HE REMINDS ME OF ANOTHER YOUNG PADAWAN FROM TATOOINE WHO WANTED TO LEARN THE WAYS OF THE FORCE.

HERA SYNDULLA

Hera Syndulla is a skilled pilot and the owner of the *Ghost*, a modified spaceship with a knack for disrupting the Empire's plans. She is a captain who takes care of both her ship and her crew of misfits. Known for being smart, savvy, and keenly aware, Hera is hard to fool. Whether she is escaping Imperial blockades or sorting out her crew's problems, Hera uses the same no-nonsense approach.

GARAZEB "ZEB" ORRELIOS

More commonly known as Zeb, this Lasat rebel is the muscle behind the crew aboard the *Ghost*. Equipped with a Lasan honor guard background, Zeb is trained to fight and survive in extreme conditions. Zeb is quick to anger and quicker to seek revenge, especially on the Empire. Now Zeb has a chance to strike back . . . and he's not going to miss.

SABINE WREN

Born on Mandalore, Sabine Wren was raised to be a warrior with an artistic twist. Armed with an arsenal of weaponry, her weapons of choice are color bombs and spray paint. Sabine is constantly trying to paint over the Empire's black, white, and gray galaxy with vivid colors. But Sabine is more than a visual artist; she's a battle expert, too. And beware any stormtroopers who cross her path, because she will draw on them like a blank canvas.

CHOPPER

Technically, this is a C1-10P astromech droid, but everyone on the *Ghost* calls him Chopper. Tasked with maintaining the ship, Chopper also sees his fair share of action. Stubborn, cranky, and a bit of a rascal, Chopper fits right in with the rest of the *Ghost* crew, though sometimes his jokes can go a little too far. Fun fact: He does not like other droids . . . at all.

BLLLLURT.

I NEVER LIKED HIM, EITHER.

EWOKS

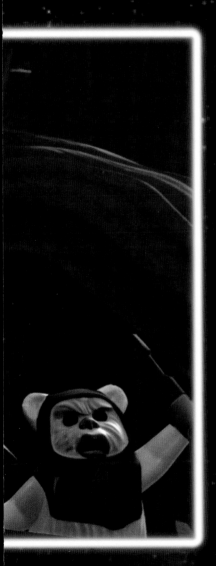

T hese furry creatures from the Forest Moon of Endor may look cute and cuddly, but they are a big pain in the neck for the Empire. With their primitive weapons of spears, slingshots, and battering rams, the Ewoks may appear to be an easy group to rule. But the truth is that they have a fierce spirit and drive to win that aligns itself with the rebels. They are expert hunters and trappers, know how to hide in the forest, and more importantly, know how to smash Imperial forces when they least expect it.

ANAKIN SKYWALKER

Dubbed the Chosen One by Qui-Gon Jinn, Anakin Skywalker is a Jedi with a great journey ahead of him. Trained by Obi-Wan Kenobi, Anakin was a devilish Padawan who always looked for action and adventure. He also fell in love with and married the brilliant Padmé Amidala. As a child he was a podracer and as a grown-up he became a great, if impulsive, Jedi. However, Anakin never felt respected by the Jedi Order and this led to very dark times in the galaxy. So dark that they made most people doubt Qui-Gon's claim. It was hard to believe that he was ever known as the Chosen One.

ANAKIN CREATED ME, AND HE WAS ALSO MY FRIEND.

THE GALACTIC EMPIRE

BOOOO! Oh, I mean, now it is time to learn about the enemies of the Rebel Alliance: **THE GALACTIC EMPIRE.** Led by Darth Sidious, the Empire is an evil organization bent on controlling the entire galaxy. The Empire wants to annihilate the Jedi Order and rule with absolute power. Anyone who dares stand up to the Empire will be brutally punished by one of its many agents of destruction.

DARTH SIDIOUS

Darth Sidious, also known as Palpatine, is the Emperor of the Galactic Empire. He is the most powerful Dark Lord of the Sith in the galaxy's history, making him and his army an Empire of unspeakable dominance. Disguising himself as an honest Senator, Darth Sidious is responsible for overthrowing both the Galactic Senate and the Jedi Order, starting the Clone Wars, and building two Death Stars. He also has a gift for swaying great warriors to the dark side, like Count Dooku and Anakin Skywalker, so beware this Sith Lord.

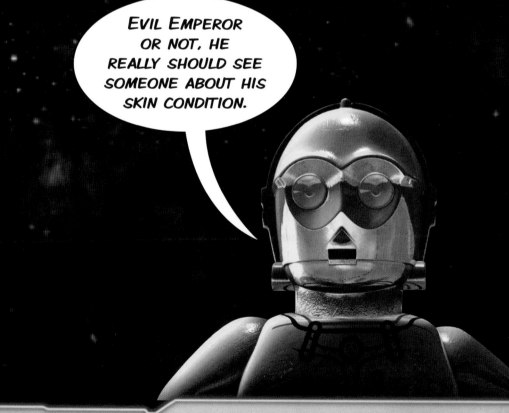

EVIL EMPEROR OR NOT, HE REALLY SHOULD SEE SOMEONE ABOUT HIS SKIN CONDITION.

DARTH VADER

It's true. Darth Vader was once a heroic Jedi Knight, but the power of the dark side drew him in and made him an evil shell of his former self. Now he leads the Empire's march to victory over the rebels, the Jedi, and whoever gets in his path. With his foreboding black mask, the mere sound of Vader's breathing strikes fear into his enemies . . . and sometimes his allies. Together with Darth Sidious, this Sith Lord ruthlessly rules with a Force-full grip.

COUNT DOOKU

Count Dooku is a corrupt Jedi who fell to the power of the dark side and became Darth Tyranus, a Dark Lord of the Sith. A dangerous fighter, Dooku is a master of deception and brute strength. Whether he is blasting starfighters with Force lightning or throttling Jedi with his dreaded Force choke, Count Dooku aims to eradicate the Jedi Order and bring the Republic to an end.

GENERAL GRIEVOUS

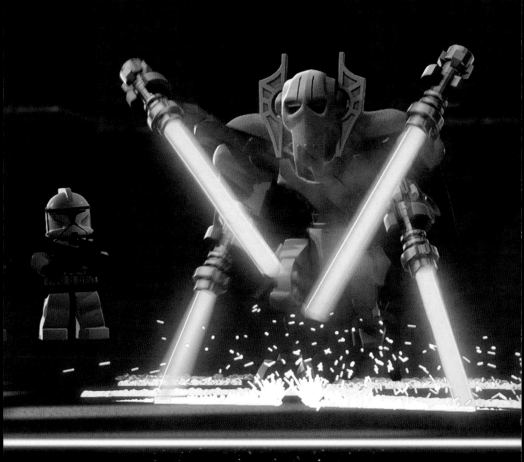

This warlord cyborg is the Supreme Commander of the Droid Army who has led many battles to victory against the Republic. He is a tactical and evil military genius who constantly outthinks and outfights his opponents with ferocious delight. Vicious and legendary, Grievous attacks with four lightsabers and no mercy.

WHAT DID OBI-WAN GIVE GENERAL GRIEVOUS?

HEART-BURN.

NUTE GUNRAY

Nute Gunray worked with Darth Sidious to invade the planet Naboo and capture Queen Amidala in order to sway the Galactic Senate's decision in a trade dispute. Fortunately, his plan did not work and the Queen escaped. Still, Gunray is a treasonous crook who secretly plotted against the Senate to help form the Separatist Army that would eventually become the Empire. Above all else, Nute Gunray is a businessman and will happily turn his back on his partners if it means making money. However, Darth Sidious knew that Gunray always puts himself first and used that fear to make Gunray do his evil bidding.

JABBA THE HUTT

Jabba the Hutt is a kingpin of crime with his slimy fingers in a number of illegal activities like gunrunning, smuggling, and gambling. With a collection of hired thugs around him at all times, Jabba is a hard Hutt to ignore. Just ask Han Solo, one of Jabba's old employees. Jabba was so angry that Han lost his payload of stolen goods that he put a bounty on Solo's head.

BOBA FETT

Raised by Jango Fett and wearing the armor of a Mandalorian warrior, Boba Fett is a bounty hunter who takes no prisoners. Boba Fett is equipped with full body armor, a rocket jet pack, and a plethora of blasters that make him a walking weapon. Boba Fett helped Darth Vader hunt down and capture Han Solo. He is sneaky, smart, and most important, reliable when it comes to evil deeds.

WHERE DID HE GET HIS DOUBLE-BLADED LIGHTSABER? AT THE DARTH SHOPPING MALL.

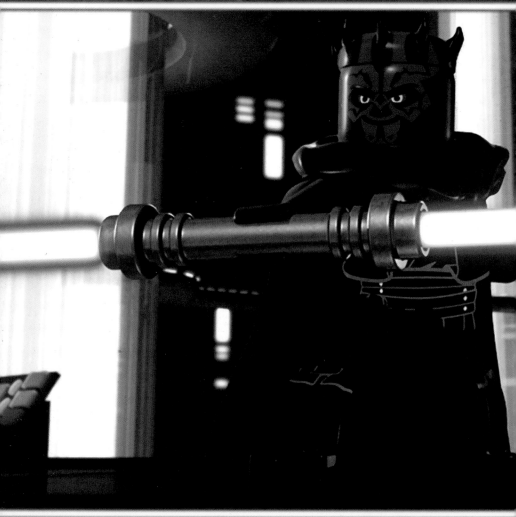

DARTH MAUL

Filled with hatred and evil, Darth Maul is one of the most dangerous and deadly Sith Lords in the galaxy. Maul was trained in the ways of the dark side of the Force by none other than Darth Sidious. With a double-bladed lightsaber at his side, Darth Maul is skilled in the awesome art of lightsaber duels and hand-to-hand combat. Ruthless, vengeful, and a little full of himself, this Sith Lord is best to avoid at all costs.

JANGO FETT

Jango Fett is regarded as one of the best bounty hunters and mercenaries in the galaxy. In fact, Jango Fett was so combat ready that he was chosen to be the genetic template for the clone troopers that became the Grand Army of the Republic in the Clone Wars . . . the same clone troopers who turned on the Jedi under Order 66. Covered in a sleek armored suit, Jango's gear includes an arsenal of weaponry from blasters to his harnessed jetpack. Now his son, Boba Fett, carries on the family name and follows in his father's dangerous footsteps.

From time to time, the Empire will hire bounty hunters to do their dirty work. These traveling mercenaries are dangerous, deadly, and will do anything for the right price.

STORMTROOPERS

Elite soldiers of the Empire, stormtroopers are the brutal might of the Imperial cause. Dressed in imposing white armor and helmets, these fighters wield blaster rifles and pistols with great skill . . . sort of. They seem to have trouble hitting targets. Stormtroopers are prone to attack in great numbers to overwhelm their enemies, so if the rebels see one, the rest of the army won't be far behind.

WHAT DID THE STORMTROOPER SAY TO HIS TARGET?

"SORRY I MISSED YOU."

SNOWTROOPERS

These are the cold weather arm of the stormtroopers, trained and prepared to battle in subzero temperatures. They are ready to chase the rebels through blizzards, hail, and over ice and snow to the end of the frozen galaxy.

BATTLE DROIDS

These are droids programmed for combat and used by the Separatist Army. They are dim-witted, suffer from multiple programming glitches, and are usually no match for Jedi Knights and clone troopers. However, when faced with an army of battle droids, the sheer number of tall, thin robotic soldiers can slow anybody down.

SEBULBA

While not technically part of the Empire, Sebulba is the archrival of a famous young podracer named Anakin Skywalker. Sebulba is a reckless racer who cheats at every turn to make sure he wins. From battering other podracers to sabotaging their equipment, no level is too low for Sebulba.

WATTO

A junk dealer on Tatooine, Watto is a real creep. A slave owner, he took possession of Anakin Skywalker and his mother. He is also a greedy, money-driven lowlife who loves to bet on podracing. He even made Anakin race for him. Luckily, Anakin was an excellent racer and, at a young age, he was able to win his freedom back from Watto. But the slave owner kept Anakin's mother. So while Watto wasn't part of the Empire, he unwittingly helped shape Anakin into the monster he would become.

WAIT, WATTO IS A JUNK DEALER? THAT'S WHERE ANAKIN REBUILT ME? AND I'M NOT JUNK . . . AM I?

BLEEEEEEP.

SPACESHIPS and VEHICLES

With all these planets being so far away from one another, both the rebels and the Empire need fast ways to get around. That's why we have spaceships and other vehicles. And of course, each spaceship serves a specific purpose, from large ones that carry tons of soldiers and weapons to small ones that are swift and nimble. I know which one is R2-D2's favorite. Care to guess?

MILLENNIUM FALCON

Piloted by Han Solo and Chewbacca, the *Millennium Falcon* is one of the fastest ships around. Used originally for smuggling, it *had* to be fast to outrace all those Imperial blockades! Armed with hyperdrive, blaster cannons, and lots of hiding places inside, with the right captain at the controls, this ship is unstoppable. Until it stops . . . then it's been known to break down every now and again.

IMPERIAL STAR DESTROYER

This giant Imperial warship lives up to its name. Designed to carry a total of 46,700 crew and 72 TIE fighters or 6 TIE squadrons, it also has 6 turbolasers, 2 ion cannons, and hundreds of other blasters aimed to ward off rebel attacks. If these spaceships are in the area, it's best to run. And don't let their large size fool you. Imperial Star Destroyers are faster than you think.

AT-AT

AT-AT is short for All Terrain Armored Transport and this machine is also known as an Imperial Walker. Not a true spaceship, the AT-AT is a heavily armed vehicle that can walk across almost any surface, making it difficult for the rebels to hide from the Empire. With its tanklike shell and many cannon blasters, AT-ATs may be slow, but they are tough to take down.

WHAT DID LUKE SKYWALKER SAY TO THE AT-AT?

"HAVE A NICE TRIP! SEE YOU NEXT FALL."

SCREEEECH.

WELL, I THOUGHT IT WAS A FUNNY JOKE.

PODRACER

A dangerous racing vehicle, the podracer is a blisteringly fast set of repulsorlift engines strapped to a one-person open-air cockpit by cables. Flying at over 450 miles an hour, these turbines drag their pilots through almost

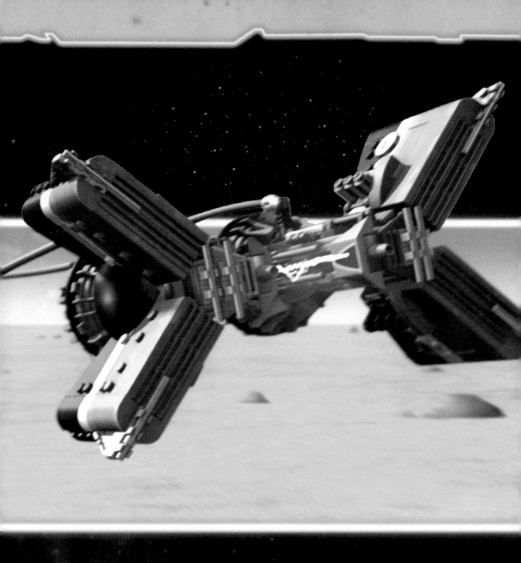

impossible race courses. And with all the other racers aiming to win any way they can, podracer pilots need to be quick to react . . . and a little bit crazy.

DEATH STAR II

The second Death Star, as with the original Death Star, is the Empire's greatest weapon. A battle station the size of a moon, it is capable of destroying entire planets with one blast of its superlaser. Protected by an energy shield and the Empire's fleet, both Death Stars are seemingly indestructible.

EXCEPT FOR THE SMALL DESIGN FLAWS THAT THE REBELS FOUND!

SLAVE I

There is nowhere to hide in the galaxy from Boba Fett and his attack craft, *Slave I*. An unusual ship, it flies in an upright position, but lands on its back. The modified starship is well armed with twin blaster cannons, two rapid-fire laser cannons, and two projectile launchers ready to blast homing missiles at anyone who dares challenge Fett.

TIE FIGHTERS

TIE fighters make up most of the Imperial Fleet. They are quick, nimble, and almost always attack in swarms. Designed to fly using the twin ion engines (or TIEs) that look like two hexagon wings on either side of the cockpit, the TIE fighters are best in close-up battles. They do not have combat shields, a hyperdrive or even a life-support system, so their pilots have to wear special suits to breathe in space. However, this makes for a lighter starfighter that can zip past rebel forces.

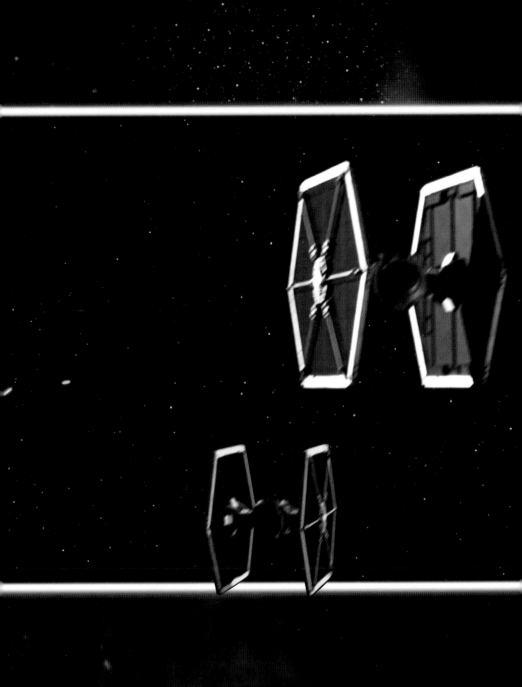

X-WING FIGHTER

The X-wing is the primary starfighter for the Rebel Alliance. It is fast, agile, and carries four laser cannons as well as dual launch tubes that fire proton torpedoes. In normal flight, the wings typically remain closed, but during battles, the wings open to form an X shape. This gives the X-wing a wider firing range for its lasers.

AT-ST

This two-legged walker is known as the AT-ST, or the All Terrain Scout Transport. Part of the Galactic Empire's fleet, the AT-ST was built for reconnaissance missions. Its light, strong frame could stand up to normal blaster fire, while its chin blasters and concussion grenade launchers are perfect for snuffing out rebels wherever they hide.

PLANETS

There are many different planets that make up the galaxy. How many would you say there are, Artoo-Detoo?

WHIRRRRR BZZZ BONP

That seems right. Which means there are many places
for the rebels to hide and many places for the Empire
to rule over. Out of these planets, a choice few became
very important battlegrounds for the war between good
and evil. They also were the places where both heroes
and villains were born.

TATOOINE

A desert planet with two suns, Tatooine wasn't just the home to scrap dealers, criminals, and moisture farmers. It was also the homeworld of Anakin Skywalker and Luke Skywalker—just not at the same time. Decades apart, Obi-Wan Kenobi trained them both in the ways of the Force, with very different results.

I FEAR I WILL NEVER GET THE SAND FROM THAT PLANET OUT OF MY GEARS!

NABOO

Visit NABOO

THE BEAUTIFUL PLANET WITH THE SILLY NAME

The rise of the Galactic Empire was due in part to three natives of beautiful Naboo: Padmé Amidala, Emperor Palpatine, and Jar Jar Binks. With grassy hills, sprawling seas, forests, mountains, and swamps, Naboo is a geographically diverse planet where both humans and Gungans reside.

HOTH

Desolately located in the Outer Rim, Hoth is an ice planet covered with snow and reaches freezing temperatures. This planet is best known for the Battle of Hoth, which resulted in a major victory for the Galactic Empire and put the rebels on ice.

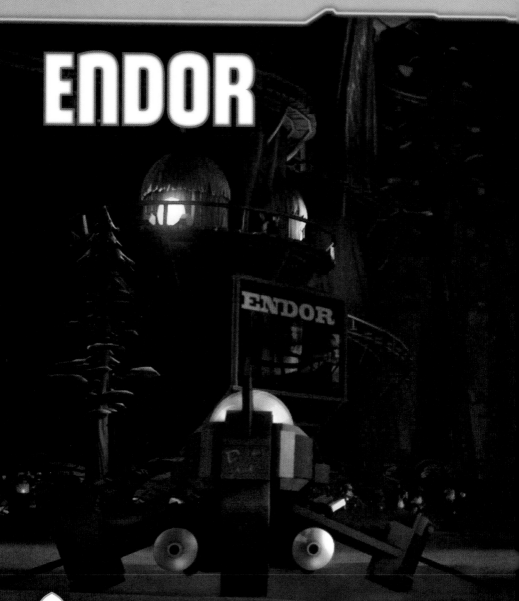

ENDOR

Also called the Forest Moon of Endor, this densely forested moon is best known as the home of the Ewoks, who played an important role in the defeat of the Empire in the Battle of Endor. Though much of its surface is heavily wooded, Endor also has small seas, deserts, mountains, and plains.

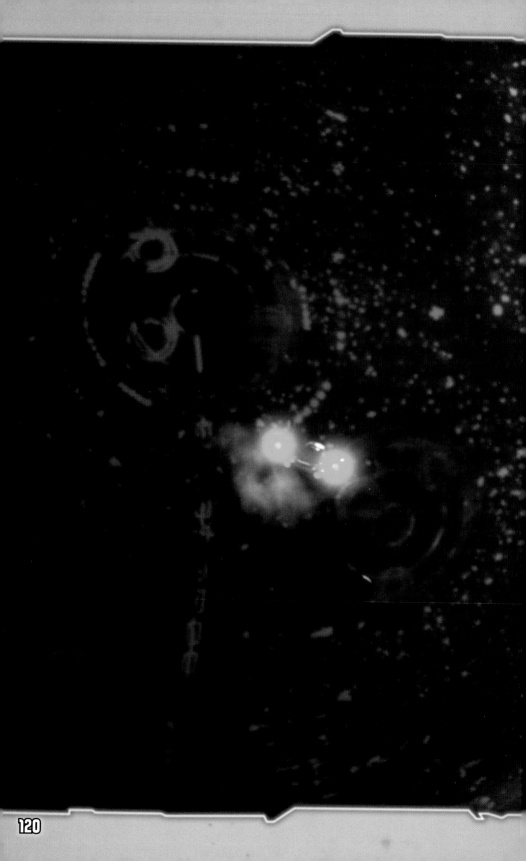

CORUSCANT

With hyperspace coordinates of (0,0,0), Coruscant is widely accepted as the de facto center of the galaxy. Serving at various times as the capital of everything from the Galactic Republic to the Empire, it also housed the Jedi Order and Jedi Academy, where Padawans trained. Coruscant's trillion residents occupy over five thousand levels. With all naturally occurring bodies of water drained to make way for more residents, artificial ecosystems were created to provide food and water.

GEONOSIS

This desert planet was the home of the Geonosians, an insectlike life-form. Geonosis was also the site of the Confederacy's first capital, and was the location of the first battle of the Clone Wars.

DAGOBAH

EVEN THE DARK SIDE OF THE FORCE WOULDN'T BE CAUGHT ON THIS PLANET.

This remote planet, located in the Outer Rim, was thick with swamps and forests, and had an unforgiving, humid climate. It was here that Jedi Grand Master Yoda served out his exile, and where he trained Luke Skywalker in the ways of the Force.

AND THAT, MY FRIENDS, IS OUR STORY. BE WELL, SAFE
TRAVELS ON YOUR NEXT ADVENTURE, AND, OF COURSE,

MAY THE FORCE BE WITH YOU.